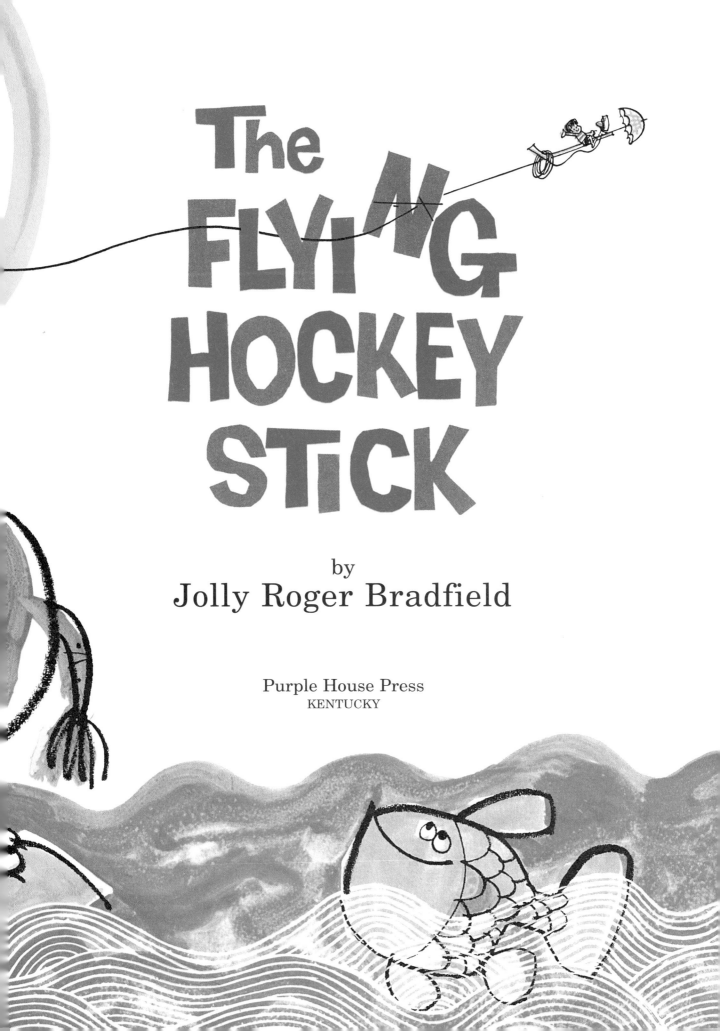

The FLYING HOCKEY STICK

by
Jolly Roger Bradfield

Purple House Press
KENTUCKY

To SIERRA
and DIEGO
GIFTS FROM GOD

Published by Purple House Press, PO Box 787, Cynthiana, KY 41031
Read about our classic children's books at www.PurpleHousePress.com and
learn more about the author at www.RogerBradfield.com

2 3 4 5 6 7 8 9 10

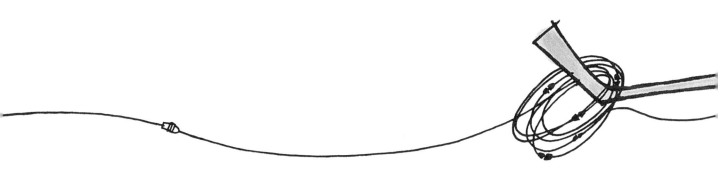

About this book

If you searched very hard and very long you might find someone (probably an adult) who didn't believe that hockey sticks could become airborne, and if you looked even harder you might find a few old curmudgeons who thought that flying hockey sticks were unsafe and should be banned.

Thankfully, Barnaby Jones had no such disabilities. His imagination knew no bounds, and he wasn't about to let a little thing like gravity interfere with his plans. (Actually, being of an age where he had yet to learn of Newton's law probably worked to his advantage.)

All children have a wonderful gift...imaginations that enable them to fight pirates and dragons, to live like royalty in beautiful castles, to discover hidden treasure. I had it when I was a child so many years ago...I could turn myself into the Lone Ranger at the drop of a Stetson.

Jolly Roger Bradfield

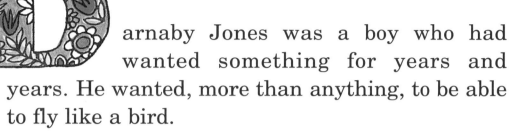

Barnaby Jones was a boy who had wanted something for years and years. He wanted, more than anything, to be able to fly like a bird.

Ever since he could remember, he had been trying to make some sort of machine that would get him off the ground, if only for a few feet.

He made a glider…but it wouldn't glide.

He made a helicopter...but it wouldn't go up.
Only down.

Barnaby had tried various combinations of orange crates, balloons, old boards, washing machine parts—and a lot of other things—but he could not seem to come up with exactly the right combination.

But (as usually happens when one keeps trying and doesn't give up) he finally found a way....

Yes, one day Barnaby hit on exactly the right parts:

One hockey stick

An electric fan

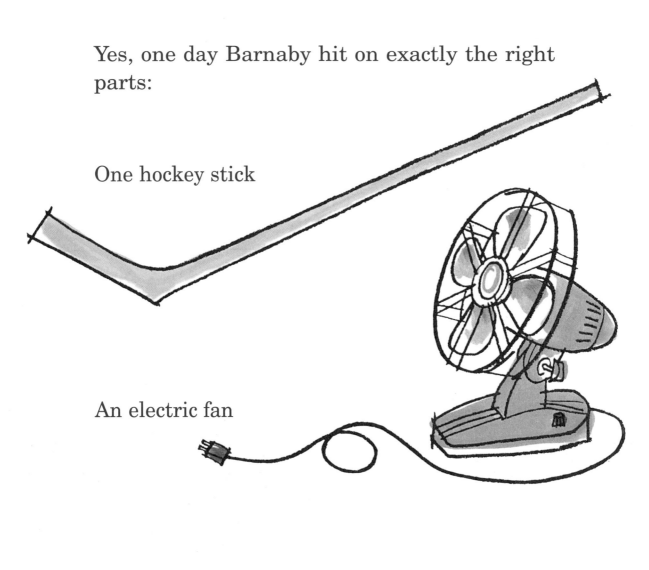

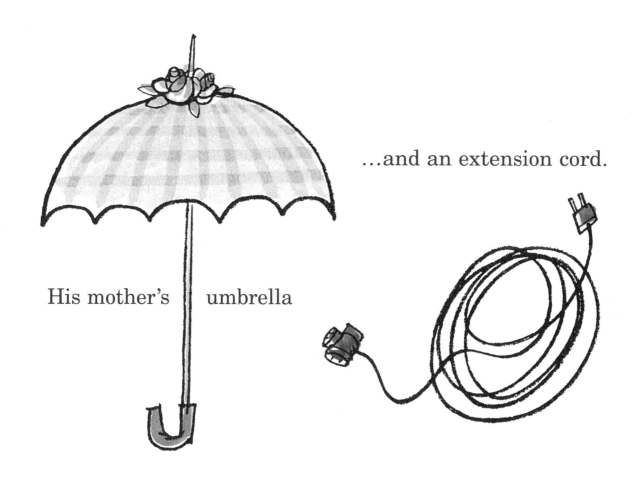

...and an extension cord.

His mother's umbrella

He taped them all together and they looked like this:

He called his invention the "Flying Hockey Stick." All he had to do to start it was to plug the cord into the socket in his bedroom, and switch on the fan!

The switch had two settings: slow and fast.
If he wanted to fly slowly, he switched the fan
to "slow." If he wanted to go faster, he merely
moved the switch.

He soon realized, of course, that in order
to fly any great distance, he would have to
have a very long cord; so he went all over the
neighborhood borrowing extension cords.

Finally he had so many strung together that it seemed to him that he would be able to fly around the world!

After testing the machine thoroughly in his back yard, he was ready to make his first long flight. Perhaps he WOULD fly around the world —if it didn't take too long.

His mother made him a lunch of peanut butter sandwiches (and a pickle) and kissed him goodbye.

The flying hockey stick worked perfectly. He switched the fan to "slow" and climbed smoothly into the air. The extension cords unwound smoothly off the back of the hockey stick as he flew along.

And, oh, what a thrill it was! He soared
to the top of a huge oak tree and peeked at a
family of birds in their nest—

He waved at a man in the window of a tall
building—

And surprised some people in an airplane.

Then Barnaby Jones spotted some smoke rising in the distance and flew toward it. Soon he could see that it came from a burning building in a nearby town.

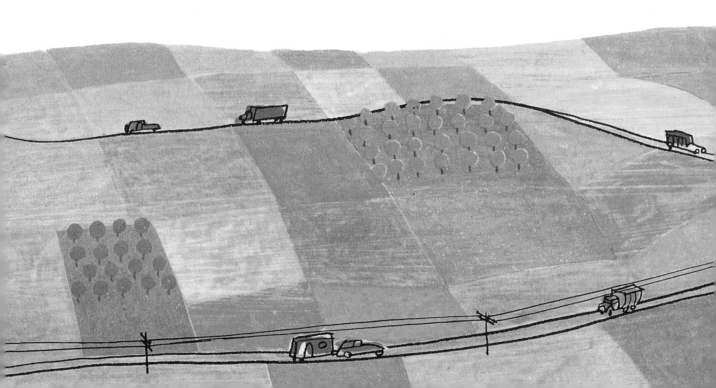

Switching the fan to "fast," he was soon at the building. In a window on the top floor was an old lady. Some firemen were trying to reach her, but their ladders weren't long enough.

"Help!" she cried. "Save me!"

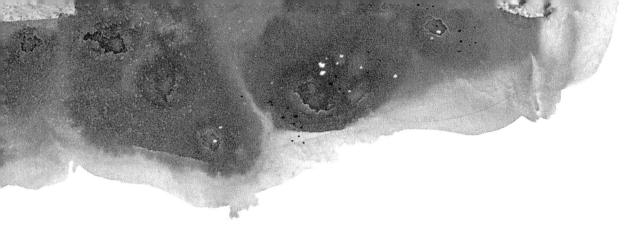

Barnaby flew up to her window.

"I can't believe my eyes, but I'm very glad to see you!" said the old lady.

"Please climb aboard, ma'am," said Barnaby politely.

The poor woman had no choice, for the flames were getting close. Putting on her Sunday hat, she climbed onto the hockey stick behind Barnaby Jones and they zoomed away.

"This is quite a contraption you have here, young man," said the old lady. After a while she added, "In fact, this is the most fun I've had in years!"

She enjoyed flying through the air so much that she decided to go with Barnaby on his trip.

They headed out across the ocean. They saw
flying fish and swimming fish.

They saw a walrus on a rock.

They saw a great whale surface and send up a
spout of water.

Flying lower to see the whale, they spotted something else in the water. It was a man clinging to a board.

"Help!" he cried. "Save me!"

Barnaby flew down to the man struggling in the water.

"I can't believe my eyes, but I'm very glad to see you!" said the man.

They hauled him aboard behind the old lady. He was the captain of a ship, who had fallen overboard at night without being noticed.

The captain asked if he could go with them

on their trip around the world. "I can help with the navigation," he said.

Barnaby didn't know what "navigation" was, but he liked the captain and welcomed him on the trip.

They flew on across the wide ocean until
they sighted land in the distance. It looked
like an island covered with dense jungle and
surrounded by a sandy beach.

As they came closer, they saw someone dash out of the jungle onto the beach. He was yelling and waving his arms.

And no wonder! He was being chased by
some very hungry-looking lions.
"Help!" he cried. "Save me!"

Once more Barnaby Jones pointed the hockey stick downward and zoomed toward the ground.

"WATCH OUT, SON," cried the captain, "WE'RE ALMOST OUT OF CORD!"

"Oh, dear," cried the old lady.

"HANG ON!" yelled Barnaby.

Barnaby zoomed in front of the lions... and at that moment they reached the very end of the cord, and stopped with a sudden jerk!

Thanks to the captain's warning, they didn't tumble off—but the old lady lost her hat, and Barnaby's lunch went spilling out onto the ground.

The lions, racing at full speed, tripped over the cord. Heads over tails they went, in a snarling tangle of teeth and tails and claws.

"I can't believe my eyes, but I'm very glad to see you," said the man on the beach; and without waiting to be asked, he jumped onto the hockey stick behind the captain.

He was a hunter who had lost his gun in
the jungle, and then had met a whole family of
hungry lions.

Barnaby Jones wheeled the hockey stick around and up into the air.

Looking down, they could see the lions eating Barnaby's peanut butter sandwiches. The hunter was glad they weren't eating *him!*

"You came along just in time!" he exclaimed. "Where were you bound for?"

"Well, we WERE going around the world, but I guess we need a little more cord," said Barnaby.

The travelers agreed that it would be best to return home, where they would all collect extension cords.

"Then we can try again!" said the little old lady, who had really enjoyed riding on the flying hockey stick.

She and the captain and the hunter were very grateful to Barnaby Jones, for he had saved their lives.

When they got back, the old lady promised to bake cookies for Barnaby every Tuesday. The sea captain made him a model ship, and the hunter gave him a huge moose head.

Now, there are some people who will tell you that Barnaby Jones just dreamed this adventure…but if you go over to his house any Tuesday, he always seems to have plenty of cookies, and there on the mantel is a beautiful model ship in a bottle, and over the mantel hangs the biggest stuffed moose head you ever saw in your whole life.